Night Running

How James Escaped
with the Help of His Faithful Dog
Based on a True Story

by Elisa Carbone

illustrated by E.B. Lewis

Alfred A. Knopf New York

Virginia, 1838 (now West Virginia)

Zeus sat looking sad and droopy as an old mule. James was fixing to run away. And then Zeus would have no one to race through the woods with at night, tracking raccoons and possums.

But James said he was done with being a slave on Master Graham's farm, and one skinny old hunting dog wasn't worth staying for. Not when there was freedom to be had.

James told his friend Levi of his secret plan to escape. Levi said he'd come, too. They'd meet in the clearing when the moon was full and follow the North Star to Canada.

James crossed his arms and looked at Zeus hard. "You're always hungry and you're noisy," he said. "I've got to leave you behind." He knelt down and scratched Zeus behind one ear. "I don't want you following me, either."

Come the night of the full moon, Zeus didn't follow. No, sir. He ran on ahead. And noisy? He made more racket than a sack of pots and pans.

"Stop barking at my friend Levi like that, you good-for-nothing hound!" James was fired-up mad.

But there was no friend in that clearing. Just the men Levi had sold James' secret to.

All Zeus could do was watch them tie James' hands behind him, watch the bald man cut a hickory switch, watch him raise that switch ready to bring it down on James' shoulders. . . .

"Aru-u-u-u-u!" Zeus howled. "Aru-u-u-u-u!"

"What's that?!" the bald man cried.

"Aru-u-u-u-u!" Zeus howled again, like cold wind through dead trees.

"A slave ghost!" the other man yelped. "Don't switch that boy, or the ghost'll come get us!"

The bald man threw that switch down like it was a rattlesnake on fire. "Master Graham can decide what to do with him come morning," he said, and spat on the ground.

Zeus snuck from tree to tree and followed. He was good at that. In the cow barn, they tied James to a milking stool, then settled in with a jug of whiskey. They passed the jug back and forth until their heads bobbed loose as puppets.

"Give some to the boy," said the bald man. "So's we can get some sleep."

They didn't see that when they poured the whiskey into James' mouth, it came right back out again and made a puddle on the barn floor. So when James fell over sideways—milking stool and all—closed his eyes, and hung his mouth open wide enough to catch mice, they thought he was out cold.

Zeus knew better.

Ropes that are slimed up with dog spit are mighty easy to untie!

"I got to run!" James whispered.

Zeus was good at that.

They ran until the sky turned pink and a new day started up. That's when James was too tired to run anymore. He burrowed under the leaves next to an old mossy log. Zeus stood guard.

Crackle, crunch, crunch.

What was that?! Zeus swung his head and growled.

"Nothing but a squirrel," James whispered. "Shhhh."

Zeus sat down.

Creak . . . creeeeeeak.

Zeus jumped up and barked.

"The trees can't even sway in the wind without you making a racket?"

James got up, angry.

"You'll get me caught, Zeus. Scat! Go home!"

But Zeus wouldn't budge.

James glanced around, scared. Nobody coming yet. But if they heard Zeus' fussing, they would be soon—with guns and whips and shackles for his feet and hands.

"If I let you live, you'll be the death of me, boy." He picked up a heavy stick to use as a club. "It's either you or me, and I've got to choose me." He raised the club, then lowered it again slowly. "Why couldn't you just keep quiet so we could hide?" James raised the club high, but he trembled all over.

"Aru—aru—aru!" The barking came from over the ridge. Slave-catcher dogs!

They came, howling and baying, with their big jaws open and teeth as sharp as broken bones.

Zeus leaped, sunk his teeth, ripped, and leaped again. James swung his club. And in one hundred seconds flat, there were no more slave-catcher dogs around to bother anyone.

But the slave catchers wouldn't be far behind.

"Zeus, *run*!" James cried.

Zeus was good at that.

They ran down into the valley and up the next mountain, until the sun was high in the sky and James couldn't run another step.

He lay down, covered himself with dry leaves, and pulled some leaves over Zeus as well.

Good thing Zeus was too tired to stand guard.

They awoke at sundown, hungry as wolves.

"Zeus, can you catch us a possum?" James asked.

Zeus was good at that.

Then they ran all night while the rest of the world slept.

They had supper at sunup (Zeus had caught two squirrels) and hid themselves so they could sleep while the sun moved across the sky.

They did that for five days and nights, until one morning they heard a rushing sound, like a rain shower sweeping through a forest, or wind coming full on up a valley. They went to have a look.

"Zeus, that's the Ohio River," said James.

They watched a steamboat glide by. It was bigger than three barns and slow and graceful as a fat lady on Sunday.

"Other side's the free state of Ohio," said James, and he sighed. Then he looked at the dark, churning water. "Wish I'd learned how to swim."

They tramped up and down the shore. "Got to be an old canoe here someplace," James mumbled.

Zeus' nose led him right to it. It had a nice rotten fishy smell.

"She's got a few holes, but I think she'll do!" James patted Zeus' head. "But"—he looked from Zeus to the boat and back again—"she's awful tippy. With you prancing around, she'll flip for sure."

He knelt down and wrapped his arms around Zeus' neck. "You been a good dog, Zeus," he said, "better than I knew a dog could be." He sniffled and wiped his nose with Zeus' ear. "Now you be free on this side of the river, and I'll be free on the other side."

James pushed the canoe from shore and paddled out into the rushing current.

Zeus watched the little boat. It bobbed and jostled. James pulled hard with his paddle.

But the boat had more than a few holes.

"Help!" James cried.

James just lay there like an old wet sock.

Zeus licked James' face and whined. But James still didn't move.

Zeus grabbed James' hand in his teeth and shook it *hard*.

"Ow!" James sat up, coughed, and spit out enough water to fill a bucket.

Zeus wagged his tail so hard his whole backside wagged along with it.

"Zeus," James said, "I won't ever try to leave you behind again!"

"Who is that trespassing on my land?" a voice boomed out.

Zeus yelped. James tried to run. But a strong hand gripped him.

"A runaway, are you, then?" The farmer looked James up and down.

James was scared silent.

"A hungry one, too, I reckon," said the farmer.

James still didn't say a word.

"Don't be afraid," said the man. "I'm a Friend. Come, my wife will fix you something to eat."

Zeus bounded along behind them.

"Git. Shoo, you mangy mutt!" The farmer swung his scythe at Zeus.

James stopped in his tracks. "Sir," he said quietly, "I mean no disrespect, but if my dog is not welcome at your house, then I'll not come, either."

The farmer raised his eyebrows so high they nearly disappeared under his hat. "That must be one mighty special dog if you're willing to give up a hot meal for him, hungry as you look."

"Yes, sir," said James. His stomach growled. "He's one mighty special dog."

The farmer's wife fixed pork stew and fresh bread for James and stale bread with pork gravy for Zeus. Then she showed them a pile of sweet-smelling hay in the barn where they could sleep. Zeus lay down on his side, so that his flank was a soft, warm pillow for James. Zeus was good at that. And they both went to sleep for the first time in a free state.

*To my neighbors and friends in Tucker County, West Virginia, who have
taught me so much about freedom and dogs.*
—E.C.

*To the students, faculty, and staff of Fleming County Schools,
Flemingsburg, Kentucky
and
To my everlasting friendship with the Emmons family:
Greg, Pam, Alexa, and Brie*
—E.B.L.

THIS IS A BORZOI BOOK PUBLISHED BY ALFRED A. KNOPF
Text copyright © 2008 by Elisa Carbone
Illustrations copyright © 2008 by E. B. Lewis
All rights reserved.
Published in the United States by Alfred A. Knopf, an imprint of Random House Children's Books, a division of Random House, Inc., New York.
KNOPF, BORZOI BOOKS, and the colophon are registered trademarks of Random House, Inc.
www.randomhouse.com/kids
Educators and librarians, for a variety of teaching tools, visit us at www.randomhouse.com/teachers
Library of Congress Cataloging-in-Publication Data
Carbone, Elisa Lynn.
Night running : how James escaped with the help of his faithful dog / by Elisa Carbone ; illustrated by E.B. Lewis. — 1st ed.
p. cm.
SUMMARY: A runaway slave makes a daring escape to freedom with the help of his faithful hunting dog, Zeus.
Based on the true story of James Smith's journey from Virginia to Ohio in the mid-1800s.
ISBN 978-0-375-82247-6 (trade) — ISBN 978-0-375-92247-3 (lib. bdg.)
[1. Fugitive slaves—Fiction. 2. Slavery—Fiction. 3. African Americans—Fiction. 4. Dogs—Fiction.] I. Lewis, Earl B., ill. II. Title.
PZ7.C1865Ni 2008
[E]—dc22
2003014502

PRINTED IN THE UNITED STATES OF AMERICA
January 2008
10 9 8 7 6 5 4 3 2
First Edition

AUTHOR'S NOTE

While researching *Stealing Freedom,* my novel about the Underground Railroad, I discovered the true story of James Smith and how his hunting dog protected him and helped him during his escape from slavery.

James was lucky that the farmer he met on the free side of the Ohio River was a Friend. "Friend" was another name for Quaker, and the Quakers were a religious group whose members often worked as abolitionists, helping slaves escape to freedom. That farmer directed James to another Friend, a farmer about thirty miles up the road. This man hired James to work on his farm. Since he'd found a place to work and live as a free person, a place where his dog was welcome, James put off traveling to Canada. James and Zeus still hunted together, though Zeus did more and more sleeping in the sun as he got older. It was on this farm that Zeus died.

James saved every penny he could, and after five years of laboring for the Quaker farmer, he bought his own farm in Huron County, Ohio. Here, while working his land, he studied and became a Baptist minister.

Seven years after James bought his farm, in 1850, the Fugitive Slave Bill was passed. This bill made it illegal for free states to harbor fugitive slaves. James heard that there was a warrant out for his arrest. Master Graham was coming to snatch Reverend James Smith back into slavery! He quickly sold his farm and fled to Canada. In Canada, he was again able to live as a free man and continue his work as a Baptist minister. Even when he grew old, James Smith still told the story about how his faithful hunting dog helped him escape from slavery.

E
C
      Carbone, Elisa Lynn.
      Night running.

DATE			